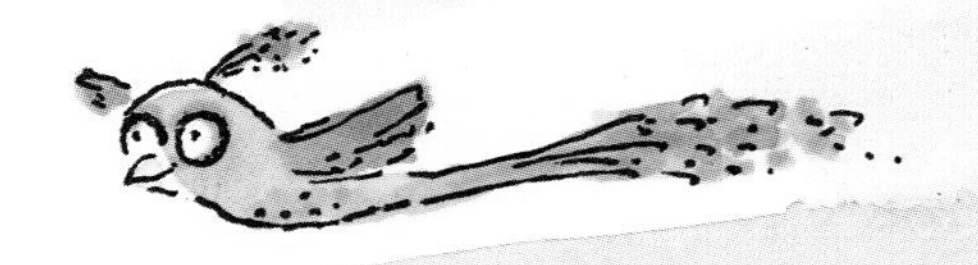

Susan Meddaugh

TREE OF BIRDS

Houghton Mifflin Company
Boston

For Poppa
and the original Birdgirl

Library of Congress Cataloging-in-Publication Data

Meddaugh, Susan.
A tree of birds / Susan Meddaugh.
p. cm.
Summary: The many friends of the wounded tropical bird Harry adopts refuse to fly south without their companion and take up residence in the tree outside Harry's bedroom window, refusing to budge even as the first snowstorm of the season approaches.
RNF ISBN 0-395-53147-0 PAP ISBN 0-395-68978-3
[1. Birds–Migration–Fiction.] I. Title
PZ7.M51273Tr 1990 89-27102
[E] – dc20 CIP
AC

Printed in the United States of America
WOZ 10 9 8 7 6 5 4 3 2

Harry didn't see the car hit the bird. He heard a soft thunk, and when he turned around, there she was. She wasn't dead, but her wing didn't look quite right, so he picked her up and carried her home.

"Oh, Mom," said Harry.
"Oh my!" said Harry's mother.
"Her name is Sally," Harry told her.

Harry took good care of Sally. He taped her wing so that it would heal. He went to the pet store and bought her food.

And he went to the library to take out some books about birds. "Did you know you're a Green Tufted Tropical?" he asked Sally. "You're supposed to be way down south this time of year. Cold weather could kill you!"

Days passed, and Sally's wing was quickly healing. But Sally stood at the window, watching the leaves fall and looking sad.

Harry's mother said, "Sally isn't eating very much."
"Maybe she's tired of worms," said Harry. "Maybe she'd like some flies for a change."
"Maybe she's lonely," said his mother.

"Sally is a wild bird," she said. "You can't keep her forever, you know. She belongs with her friends."

"I'm her friend," said Harry.

The next day, Harry had the strangest feeling that he was being followed. But every time he turned around, no one was there.

That afternoon, he noticed something unusual outside his window.
While all the other trees were losing their leaves,
one tree was getting greener and greener. Bright tropical green.
Harry went outside to investigate.

When he got close to the tree he saw that it wasn't covered with leaves. It was a tree full of birds—Green Tufted Tropicals, just like Sally.

They made Harry uncomfortable,
so he went back into the house.

The next morning the birds followed Harry to school.

They waited for him outside,

and when school was over,
they followed him home.

Every night the birds perched in the tree outside Harry's window. Every day they followed him everywhere he went. Harry knew what they wanted. "You can't have Sally," he told them.

The days got colder. The birds stayed on. It seemed that nothing would convince them to fly south. Not wind.

Not rain.

Not Harry himself. But he tried.

First he tried to reason with them. "Sally is my bird," he explained. "I'm taking good care of her, so you can all go now." The birds didn't go anywhere.

Harry tried to frighten the birds away.

The birds were not fooled.

Harry pleaded with them: "Don't you know winter is coming? You've got to fly south before it's too late. You'll never survive the first snowstorm!"

Still the birds wouldn't leave.
As the days grew colder, Harry found himself checking the thermometer and listening to the weather reports. Then one morning, Harry heard the words he had been dreading. "Get out your snow shovels," said the weatherman. "A big winter storm is coming our way!"

Harry ran outside. The sky was definitely winter gray. The temperature was definitely dropping. And the Green Tufted Tropicals were turning blue.

"This is your last chance!" he yelled at the tree of birds.
"Get out now before it snows!"
He shook a stick at the tree.
He threw a rock.

Not one bird moved.

"STUPID, STUPID BIRDS!" he screamed. "Don't blame me if you all freeze to death."

Harry went to his room with a heavy heart.
He saw Sally looking out at the tree of birds.
"Oh, Sally," Harry said. "Do you miss your friends so much?"

At that moment a single snowflake fell past Harry's window.

Harry knew what he had to do.
He opened the window . . .

"Oh, Mom!" said Harry.